# A Season to Bee

# A stylish book of colors

## WRITTEN AND ILLUSTRATED BY CARLOS APONTE

PRICE STERN SLOAN · AN IMPRINT OF PENGUIN RANDOM HOUSE

PRICE STERN SLOAN
Penguin Young Readers Group
An Imprint of Penguin Random House LLC

Copyright © 2017 by Carlos Aponte. All rights reserved. Published by Price Stern Sloan, an imprint of Penguin Random House LLC, 345 Hudson Street, New York, New York 10014. *PSS!* is a registered trademark of Penguin Random House LLC. Manufactured in China.

*Library of Congress Cataloging-in-Publication Data is available.*

ISBN 9781101995709      10 9 8 7 6 5 4 3 2 1

This book is dedicated to the little ones I know,
Sole Luka, Dylan, Valentina, Joaquin, Hudson, Violet,
Delphine, Delilah, Dashel, Ruby, Rowan, and specially
to my godson Leone and goddaughter Cameron

—CA

It's spring in the meadow,
time to shake off the freeze.
What's the new look from
the flowers and the trees?

*Click, click, click,* go the bugs in high heels,
all waiting to see what the catwalk reveals.

"It's a season to BEE!" exclaims Miss V. McQueen, editor of *BUZZ* fashion magazine.

"What should we wear?" ask the six-legged press.
"Who should we follow and how should we dress?"

"I have a question about the new trends!"
says a small fashion bug with a big camera lens.
"Which colors are best for this season to be?"

"Quick!" says McQueen. "Follow me!"

"BEE bold like the sun
that melts snow . . .
wear
GOLD!"

"Feel light, like the clouds in the sky . . . wear

# WHITE!"

"Stop 'em dead like the ladybug
in spring . . . wear
**RED!**"

"To look stylish and clean . . .

you should be wearing

# GREEN!"

"Say it with a wink, feel chic . . .

wear PINK!"

"Style it like the iris in the field . . . add some VIOLET!"

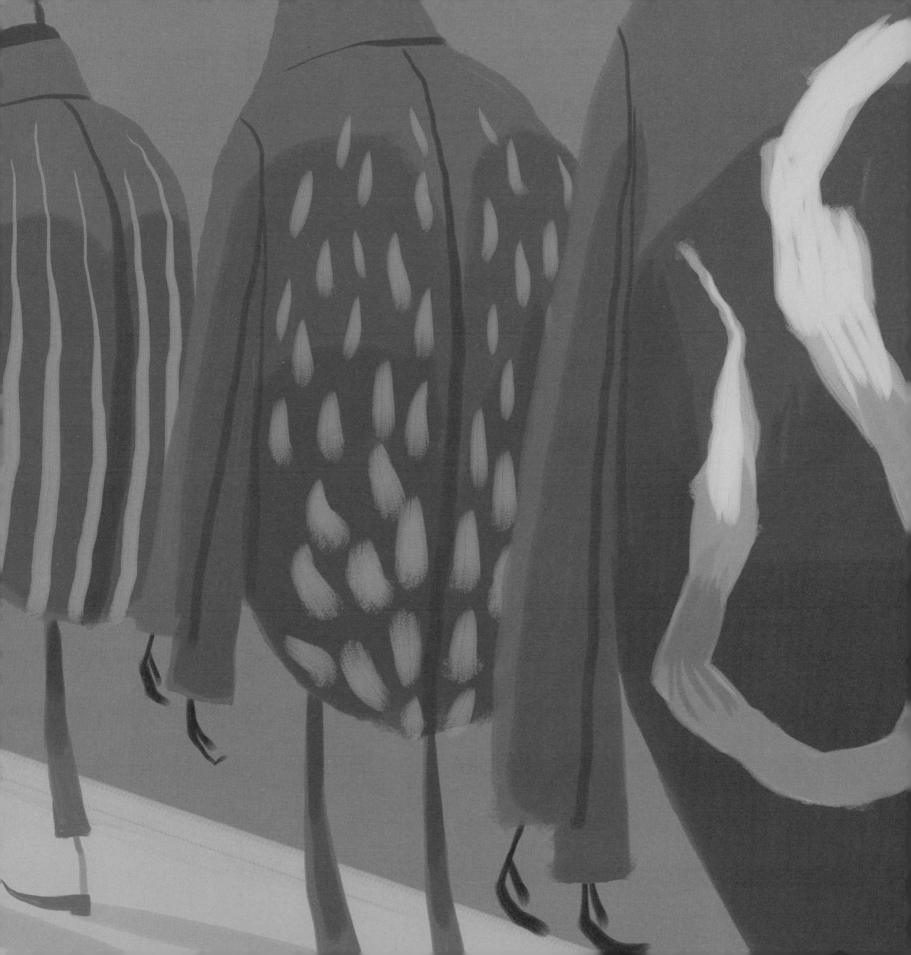

"Stay true, like the color of the sky . . .

wear BLUE!"

"BEE posh,
front to back,
like the spider . . .

wear

BLACK!"

"Miss V," says the fashion bug,
"so much to see!
What's the most important
thing of all to be?"

"In the spring, summer, fall, and winter, too—
the most important thing to BEE is . . .

YOU!"

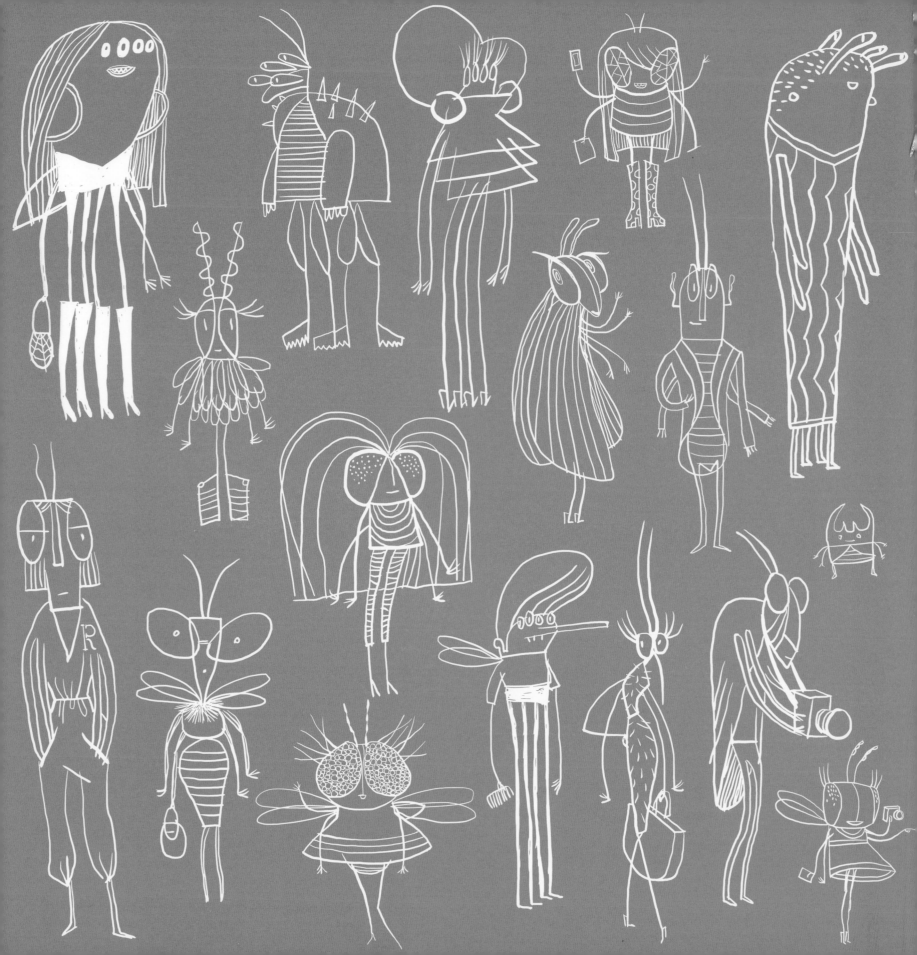